2 tales of 2 dogs

By Michael McCarthy

Illustrated by Rob Bennett

AuthorHouse™
1663 Liberty Drive
Bloomington, IN 47403
www.authorhouse.com
Phone: 1-800-839-8640

© 2010 Michael McCarthy. All rights reserved.

No part of this book may be reproduced, stored in a retrieval system,
or transmitted by any means without the written permission of the author.

First published by AuthorHouse   10/29/2010

ISBN: 978-1-4520-7722-2 (sc)

Printed in the United States of America
Bloomington, Indiana

This book is printed on acid-free paper.

Adventure in Hawkstone Follies

Woodstock and Churchill are two mischievous dogs. Woodstock is a shiny black Labrador, and Churchill is a shaggy Golden Retriever. They love to spend many hours playing around in the mysterious rocks, bushes and strange buildings at the famous Hawkstone park in Shropshire.

One day the two friends are at the park as usual. They are being taken for a walk by their owner, Charlie the farmer. Suddenly they spot something very odd...

A WHITE RABBIT!

Immediately they both decide to chase after the rabbit. The frightened rabbit starts to run. The faster the rabbit runs, the faster Woodstock and Churchill run. Eventually the furry, white animal vanishes down a hole, and without thinking Woodstock and Churchill follow until they also completely disappear from view.

Eventually the two dogs find themselves in a dark, eerie cave. Although they feel a little afraid, they bravely carry on running, determined to follow the rabbit. On and on they go - deeper and deeper underground, until they soon realise they are lost in this murky, wet, cold place! They are just beginning to panic when all of a sudden they see a flicker of light in the distance. Woodstock barks at Churchill:-

"Come on old boy let's follow the light"

With some relief they start scampering towards the glimmer of light hoping they're soon going to find their way out, when without warning a rush of water from an underground stream comes cascading towards them. They blink in amazement as the water runs into their eyes. In their confusion they don't know which way to turn and begin barking to each other in dismay.

All at once the two dogs catch sight of the bobbing white tail of the rabbit in front of them.

"Look Woodstock," barks Churchill,

"It's the rabbit-let's go!"

As they try to keep up with the zigzagging of the frisky white animal in front of them, they find themselves moving away from the torrent of water. They stop for a moment to shake the water from their damp fur coats and manage to send all the underground insects scurrying to find somewhere to hide!

Up and up the intrepid explorers climb, hoping they will soon find a way out. They seem to be going round and round in circles! On and on they climb, higher and higher. Suddenly as if by magic they shoot out into dazzling sunshine, and find themselves.......

in the middle of Hawkstone golf course!

A golfer who has been about to strike the ball from there nearly jumps out of his skin. He cannot not believe what he is witnessing - two large dogs flying out of the 14th hole! Is he dreaming or just seeing things?

Woodstock and Churchill are also amazed – they wonder how on earth they managed to get here.

The two friends take one look at the shocked and bewildered golfer and decide to make a run for it!

"Let's get out of here!" barks Churchill to Woodstock.

"Yes we'd better scarper!" yelps Woodstock in agreement.

The two adventurous dogs speed off in the direction of the magnificent Hawkstone Hall. Two bored green keepers spot them and start to give chase. One of the keepers is tall and gangly, the other short and stocky. Suddenly the shorter one trips over a stray golf ball, causing the tall guy to crash into him. They both end up in a heap on the ground feeling bruised and dazed.

On and on run Woodstock and Churchill, getting closer and closer to Hawkstone Hall. As they scurry through the gravel surrounding the great building, they are drawn towards the massive front door which has been left wide open. The two mischievous dogs run straight through it and into the grand hallway, where they come to a sudden.....**HALT!**

In front of them stands a man dressed in long flowing robes. The mysterious figure is none other than Father Dennis, the head priest at Hawkstone Hall. He is astonished to see the two panting creatures skidding to a standstill on the highly polished hall floor. Woodstock and Churchill are also very surprised and a little scared.

"Come on," yelps Woodstock, **"Let's skedaddle,**

We need to find our way back."

They turn and shoot through the door, churning up the beautiful, well kept lawns as they go.

"Stop you rascals!" Father Dennis shouts after them; but they take no notice

and keep on running. They run and run until they are exhausted. When they finally stop, they realise they are at the bus stop in the nearby village of Marchamley. Suddenly to their amazement a large blue vehicle appears from round the bend. As it is chugging towards them, Woodstock barks,

"Hey it's a bus, let's get on-it may take us home."

When the bus stops, the two crazy dogs jump on quickly and scamper to the back, in a blur of black and gold.

The driver and the passengers are so shocked they are speechless. In a daze the driver decides to carry on and see what happens next. The bus twists and turns along the narrow lanes. The two friends begin to enjoy the ride, and put their front paws up on the window, so they can watch passing traffic and spot other dogs they know walking obediently with their owners!

Eventually the bus comes to a juddering standstill, right outside the grand Hawkstone golfing hotel. Before anyone has time to blink, Woodstock and Churchill have jumped off and are away.

Soon they find themselves back on the golf course

face to face with the unlucky golfer who had been so astonished earlier when they had magically flown out of the now destroyed 14th hole.

He is so surprised to see them again that he manages to swipe the golf ball right out of the bunker he has been stuck in since their first arrival. The two dogs bark:

"Well done!"

to the unfortunate man, who is by now in such a state of shock, he faints clean away!

Fortunately Charlie the farmer spots his two wayward charges and runs up to them shouting:-

"Where have you been, and what have you been up to- you mad pair?"

Woodstock and Churchill stare at Charlie in bewilderment.

"We don't know how it all happened , but we're very hungry and thirsty" they whimper.

Charlie brings the unconscious golfer round and makes sure that he is feeling better before they all go back to the hotel for refreshment, and to recount their adventures to all their doggy and human friends.

The End

Adventure in Shrewsbury Castle

It is a warm spring morning in May, and Woodstock and Churchill are with their owner Charlie the farmer in their favourite place-Hawkstone park. They are very excited by the smells and sounds of the spring, and Woodstock is getting quite dizzy running around in circles chasing his own tail. Churchill, who has wandered off following a very interesting scent, suddenly spots a delivery van parked near the hotel.

"**Look Woodstock**" barks Churchill "**that van is going to Wem-why don't we hitch a ride?**"

Woodstock replies: "**Yes quick-Charlie's talking to the driver-we've got a chance to jump in!**"

They skip into the back of the van unseen by the two men. After what seems ages, the driver gets in and starts the engine. The dogs shiver with excitement as the van moves off, but manage to sit quietly so as not to be discovered. Quite soon the van slows down and comes to a standstill. The two daring dogs look at one another and jump out quickly.

"Thanks for the lift mate!" they bark to the very surprised driver, who watches them run off with his mouth open in shock.

They are just wondering where they are when a fast train roars past on the nearby railway line. They are at Wem station! The brilliant idea strikes them both at the same time-

"Let's get the train to Shrewsbury" they bark excitedly to each other.

They know that they will have to hide somewhere on the train, as they have no money for the train fare.

A few minutes later a big green train jolts to a halt at the platform. The two dogs jump on quickly- much to the surprise of the other passengers.

They make their way to the guard's van and look for somewhere to hide. They find a pile of boxes and manage to wriggle their way into the middle so as not to be seen.

"This is great fun," whispers Churchill to Woodstock –

"I hope we make it to Shrewsbury without being found!"

Just as they disappear out of sight, a guard comes in the van and thinks he sees two boxes moving by themselves.

"I must need a holiday" he mumbles to himself.

A while later the dogs are getting restless. They are beginning to think they will not be able to stop themselves bouncing about or barking, when at last they hear the announcement for Shrewsbury station

" Phew, thank goodness!" mutters Woodstock as together they make a run for it and bound off the train in one huge **L-L-EAP!**

The poor guard who thought he saw boxes moving in the van now can't believe he is seeing two large dogs jumping off his train.

"**I definitely need a holiday**" he sighs, scratching his head in confusion.

The two dogs make their way up castle hill – very pleased with themselves for getting this far. At the top of the hill they notice a sign saying:

'SHREWSBURY CASTLE'

" **YE-E-S!" Let's go**" they bark.

It is still a fine spring day and Woodstock and Churchill are attracted by all the new, tantalising smells of the castle grounds. They bounce around enthusiastically following all sorts of trails, when they suddenly find themselves at the edge of a large pond.

"**Look Churchill there's a big fat water rat**" barks Woodstock

"**Wow**" yelps Churchill, "**let's swim after it**"

Without another thought, they launch themselves into the pond with a tremendous **SPLASH!** They quickly locate the large furry brown rat again and start swimming after it. After a few minutes of giving chase the rat seems to disappear into a hole in the bank.

Woodstock and Churchill investigate the hole and find themselves entering into what seems to be some sort of dark tunnel. As their eyes start to become accustomed to the gloom they realise they are in an old, narrow, smelly passageway with the remains of peeling yellow paint and candle wax on the walls. The walls are also slimy and dripping with icy water. On the floor are traces of rush matting. This was obviously once a well used route.

"**I wonder if this is a secret passage to the castle**" exclaims Churchill in awe.

"**Wow, come on let's explore**" answers Woodstock gleefully.

After a few minutes Woodstock bumps into something, and straining to see, they realise they have reached what seems to be the end of the passageway. There are three worn stone steps, leading to an ancient, heavy oak door held together with metal studs.

"**I wonder what's behind the door**" Woodstock asks in rather a scared voice.

"**Don't be frightened old boy, help me push and we'll find out!**" replies Churchill cheerfully.

They both put all their weight against the door and it slowly begins to open inch by inch, so that there is just enough room for the two dogs to squeeze through. They find themselves in what seems to be a large cellar. It smells very musty, and by the small amount of light coming in from a tiny window, they see that the room is full of old junk. There are suits of armour, old furniture and interesting looking boxes. They are thrilled, and have great fun investigating the boxes.

One box is full of old clothes, hats and shoes. They decide to try on some hats. They look very strange wearing extravagant ladies hats, adorned with feathers and ribbons!

When they finish exploring, they see another half open door leading out of the cellar.

"**That must lead to the castle**" barks Churchill "**let's go and find out.**"

They bound through the door still wearing their hats and find themselves in a comfortable lounge with the television on, showing the local news.

Suddenly they see two very familiar looking dogs on the screen.

"**That's us!** bark the pair of them together, **and there's Charlie**"

Charlie is saying on the programme that he is upset to have lost his two dogs. Suddenly a man in a smart uniform enters the lounge. He is extremely surprised to see two large dogs wearing old fashioned hats staring at the television. He glances at the screen and realises with amazement that the two missing dogs on the news item are standing in front of him!

"**Qui-i-ck-let's scarper!**" barks Churchill, as he realises they have been recognised. The two friends take to their heels and run further into the castle. They pass startled tourists who are looking around the ancient building, and panic starts to set in as they scamper through endless rooms and corridors.

"**Are we ever going to get out of here?**" they wonder.

Suddenly they spot a lift in a hallway.

They decide to hop in and get a ride up to the roof! They press the big red button, and with some relief feel the lift shooting upwards. The doors open slowly when they reach the roof and the two dogs stroll out. They are just admiring the breathtaking view across the rooftops of Shrewsbury town when they hear voices approaching.........

In a panic the two dogs run round madly trying to find a way off the roof. Luckily they quickly find the fire escape leading down the side of the castle, and without wasting another second they fling themselves onto it, scramble quickly down the metal staircase and are soon back on firm ground.

Now that they seem to be safe and free, they start to run. They just keep running and running in what they hope is the direction of home.

After a few miles they gradually start trotting slower and slower. They are becoming more and more tired, thirsty and hungry. Suddenly they hear a squeal of brakes. They look round and see that a very well known landrover has stopped next to them.

"**It's Charlie!**" barks Woodstock with joy.

The landrover door opens quickly and an angry looking Charlie gets out and marches towards them. "**Have you been up to your tricks again?**" he shouts.

The two dogs look very dejected, with drooping ears and their tails down. Charlie sees how exhausted they are and softens. "**Come on then you scallywags, let's get you into the landrover and home.**"

The two shattered dogs manage to climb in and settle down on their comfy blanket in the back of the vehicle. A few minutes later the sound of gentle snoring reaches Charlie, and he smiles to himself - glad to have his two mischievous charges back safely.

Very soon Charlie turns into his drive and with great difficulty rouses the two worn out dogs from their dreams. They go into the warm house and enjoy a scrumptious meal together. All wolf down their favourite food of sausages- but Charlie has chips and peas with his!

When all food and drink has gone, the three settle down in front of the roaring fire and drift slowly off to sleep.

Michael asked,"How can I be famous like Roald Dahl "?

"You need to write a book first Mike" was the reply.

Here we have his first step to fame, "Two Tales of Two Dogs".

Michael is registered blind, hemi-plegic and has learning difficulties. The stories are another strand of Michael's determined character to achieve. Learning to walk again, climbing mountains, completing marathons or riding a bike coast to coast are routine achievements, the book is something special.

The stories are Michael's original ideas told to Anne-Marie a friend who completed the London Marathon with Michael and Catherine a neighbour who has worked closely with Michael over the years. The team was completed when Rob Bennett, another neighbour, joined as the illustrator.

Churchill a golden Labrador was Michael's dog and Woodstock was owned by Mr Jarvis, Michael's headmaster at Condover RNIB School. The other main character Charlie is a neighbouring farmer.

Thank you for reading Michael's book and if you have enjoyed it, have any comments or wish to be put on the mailing list for the next one
please email Michael:

mgm@talk21.com.

Ps

The next story is flying off the pages!!!

Rob Bennett illustrations and character sculpted figures

Tel: 01939 200634   www.robbennett.org

LaVergne, TN USA
18 November 2010
2041LVUK00002B